Stone Age, Historical Tales

Historical Tales, Volume 1

Alexeyev K. Zurga

Published by Time Traveler Zurga's Press, 2024.

This is a work of fiction. Similarities to real people, places, or events are entirely coincidental.

STONE AGE, HISTORICAL TALES

First edition. July 13, 2024.

Copyright © 2024 Alexeyev K. Zurga.

ISBN: 979-8227264466

Written by Alexeyev K. Zurga.

Introduction

WELCOME TO THE FASCINATING world of the Stone Age, a time filled with mysteries and discoveries that laid the foundations of human civilization! Within the pages of this book, you will encounter captivating stories of courage, ingenuity, and adventure, all set in this distant era. While the characters and actions are born of imagination, each story is followed by a brief summary revealing well-documented historical truths.

This unique combination of fiction and reality aims to provide a reading experience that is not only enjoyable but also educational. The stories will take you into dark, vast caves, across wild plains, and into primitive villages, where you will discover how our distant ancestors lived, worked, and dreamed. Each story will enrich your knowledge of this fascinating era, familiarizing you with important historical concepts and events.

By reading these tales, you will not only be transported to a long-gone world, but you will also learn new things about the beginnings of humanity. I invite you to join our heroes on their journeys, to learn alongside them, and to enjoy the beauty of history presented in an accessible and charming manner.

Masti the Mastodon: A Prehistoric Adventure

IN THE EARLIEST DAYS of the world, before humans walked the earth, there existed a time of pristine beauty and natural abundance. It was a world untouched by human hands, where the land stretched far and wide, adorned with lush forests, winding rivers, and majestic mountains. Life flourished in abundance, with magnificent creatures roaming freely and the air filled with the sweet scent of blooming flowers. In this idyllic paradise, the cycle of life unfolded with effortless grace, setting the stage for the dawn of humanity. The world was vastly different from today; it was home to species of animals that no longer exist today, such as dinosaurs, mastodons, and mammoths. Masti's story takes place in these very, very distant times. It's known as the prehistoric era, the period when Masti lived.

Prehistory refers to the time before written records, when there were no books or documents to chronicle the past. It's the epoch when humans existed, but written language hadn't yet been developed.

History, on the other hand, pertains to the era in human history where written records are present. During this time, without the means of writing, people engaged in various activities such as hunting, fishing, and gathering fruits, seeds, roots, and edible plants. As time progressed, they also began to adopt agriculture and the domestication of animals. But for now, let me share Masti's story with you.

In prehistory, there lived a couple of mastodons who couldn't have a child. They belonged to the large family of Anancus mastodons, named Anancus for their straight tusks, almost vertical, unlike today's mammoths or elephants. However, this couple eventually had a son, the sweetest little elephant, with wide ears, sparkling eyes, and a gentle voice. They named him Little Masti and took great care of him, cherishing him dearly.

As he grew a little older, Masti loved to wander everywhere, and he befriended an old pike who had a habit of spinning all sorts of tall tales and fantastic stories, as if they were real events. Masti found amusement in his rich imagination and the way he told his tales.

Once, he lied, saying that last night he grew two legs and danced with a little girl to the music of bird chirps. Another time, he claimed that in his youth he had wings, flew far away from here, and met dinosaurs; he barely escaped with his life, but they sent him back because they couldn't stand how much he talked. Masti found it amusing; he knew that dinosaurs had died out a long time ago. He had heard from his grandfather that they once existed, but he couldn't have met them. Maybe in dreams. He also lied that last year he went to an animal masquerade ball, dressed so beautifully that he was mistaken for the king of elephants and placed on the throne, while the real elephant king was chased away because he dressed as a dog. And he, the new king, immediately waged war with the Borsoni mammoths and punished them for trying to steal the food of the mastodons. Such stories he invented every day, presenting them as if they were true.

Masti found great amusement in each encounter, but his parents scolded him many times for this friendship. They said, "Why doesn't he choose a friend who lives on land, like us? If not a mastodon, at least a tapir, a wild pig, an antelope, or a horse, not a deceitful old pike living in the water." But Masti didn't listen to them because he loved the pike dearly, even though he was otherwise a very obedient child.

Once, Masti went out for a walk but didn't return. His parents waited for him, but as it started to get dark, they grew worried and began searching everywhere. They ran into the forest, but he wasn't there. They dashed to the neighboring hills, but he wasn't there either. They went to the lake where he used to bathe, but he wasn't there either. They asked the wild pigs, but they didn't know. They asked the tapirs, but they didn't know either. They asked the fish, but no one knew anything about Masti.

Until they met a bird named Petu, who had seen him drowning in the lake.

The parents became even more frightened, but they immediately rushed to that place. On the way, they asked Petu if he had helped Masti, but he laughed at them.

-How could I, a tiny bird, help an elephant??!

-But why didn't you come and tell us, so we could help?!

-Oh, why should I bother for nothing? He probably drowned by the time I got to you. Better not waste my effort.

The poor parents were so distraught and sad that they didn't say anything anymore. They just wanted to get to the lake as quickly as possible, hoping that maybe he had somehow escaped. When they arrived at the spot indicated by Petu, indeed, their son was there, nearly fainting from exhaustion but alive!!!

Their joy knew no bounds! They kissed him, caressed him, and cried tears of happiness at finding him alive. Masti recounted to them how he had entered the lake in a spot he had never ventured before, and it seemed everything alright. But after a few steps, he began sinking into the marsh, with nothing to hold onto to save himself. He was so frightened that he began to scream, and his friend, the old pike, heard him and immediately came to his rescue. Not just him, but he quickly summoned all the pikes in the lake, who together created such a huge wave that it threw him onto the shore.

Can you imagine how grateful Masti's parents were now to this old, deceitful pike because he had just saved their son's life?! Since then, they have never scolded Masti for this friendship and have generously rewarded all the pikes in that lake. And so, with Masti's safe return, the family celebrated their reunion, cherishing the bond that had grown stronger through the trials of their unforgettable adventure in the prehistoric world.

This story was inspired by the world's most complete skeleton, the Mastodon Anancus Arvernensis, located in Baraolt, a small town in

Romania. The characters and story are fictional, but four historical truths are worth noting: at the beginning of the earth, there was no human presence, only plants and animals. Historians generally consider prehistory as the time before written records, while history refers to the period with written records. Prehistoric animals include the Mamuth Borsoni, Mastodon Anancus Arvernensis, and Southern Mammoth, all of which lived long after the dinosaurs. Prehistoric humans lived by hunting, fishing, and gathering seeds, plants, and roots, later transitioning to agriculture and animal domestication.

Leyla and the Domestication of Goats

CLIMATE CHANGE, SUDDEN warming or cooling of temperatures, as well as changes in precipitation patterns, have contributed to major changes in society. Rising temperatures, for example, lead to rising sea levels, and high temperatures can cause drought and desertification, as happened in the case of the Sahara and the Arabian Peninsula.

Some archaeologists say that people have become better at building new things and using better tools, and that has helped us progress and have a better life. Therefore, they divide history into epochs such as the Stone Age and the Metal Age. However, perhaps the greatest change in human life was their transition from being hunter-gatherers to cultivating plants and domesticating animals. That's why they also divided the Stone Age into several parts, such as the Paleolithic, Mesolithic, and Neolithic.

Their gradual transition from hunter-gatherers, with an intermediate stage of plant caretakers and protectors, to plant cultivators and animal domestics, was therefore essential. It's quite easy to understand what it means to be a hunter-gatherer, but we might wonder what it means to be a caretaker and protector of animals in the Stone Age. Well, let me provide an example to make it clearer. For instance, Native Americans in North America didn't sow seeds or plant anything, but they facilitated the growth of certain species favorable to them. Concerning animals, they didn't yet domesticate them, but they had the habit of not hunting female animals, pregnant ones, or young specimens to avoid endangering the species. That's what it meant in the Stone Age to care for animals in this regard. Today I will tell you a story set in the Stone Age, towards the end of a period called the Neolithic, about how a dear and adorable girl named Leyla domesticated a goat.

Leyla and her family lived in a mountainous area with cooler winters and milder summers, somewhere in what is now Iran, not far from desert regions characterized by hot and dry summers. The goats loved the mountainous areas, and their presence provided an important resource for her family as hunting objects. Everyone ate their meat, except Leyla. Even at a young age, she noticed something peculiar. She was so perceptive that she couldn't even speak yet, but she observed that when animals were killed, they cried out and made sounds of pain. With her childlike mind, she concluded that animals didn't like being hurt. As compassionate as she was, she refused to eat any kind of meat. Not even fish.

One day, her father and older brother went out hunting, as they usually did. They had quite some success quickly, hunting down a goat, but as soon as they killed it, they noticed that the nanny goat had two fairly large kids. Without much thought, they decided to hunt down these two kids as well, but they realized they couldn't use all that meat at once. So, to prevent the meat from spoiling, they thought to themselves that they should only injure the kids enough to capture them so they could take them home. After they finished the mother goat's meat, they could then kill the kids one by one, ensuring they'd have plenty of meat for a long time. And so, with a nod and some silent signals, father and son managed to catch the two young goats easily. Proud and pleased, they headed home with their catch, barely able to carry them both.

At home, the woman rejoiced at the meat, while Leyla cherished the adorable little goats that had stolen her heart from the first moment. She pleaded with her parents to let her take care of them, to feed them, and to clean the space where they'd be kept, and her parents agreed. Leyla fed them 2-3 times a day, changed their water daily, and even gave them a large chunk of salt because goats enjoy and need to lick salt regularly. But she also talked to them and petted them, and they became the best of friends.

They lived beautifully, in greater happiness, for a while, but then came the day when Leyla's parents decided it was time to slaughter one of the goats. It was a rainy, rather cold day. Leyla's father had no desire to go hunting, her mother didn't feel like going out to gather edible plants in such ugly weather, and at home, they didn't have much to eat. As they were about to start their tasks, Leyla, understanding what was happening, burst into indescribable tears, then she screamed! The quiet and smiling girl turned into a true fury! Her cheeks turned red, her hand trembled, and she screamed at the top of her lungs that she would not let them kill her best friends.

Leyla's parents were shocked to see her like this; they didn't know what to say, so surprised were they. They remained silent for a few moments, and it was the first time they didn't scold the girl when they didn't agree with her. They left the goats alone, they didn't eat anything that day. After that scene, the question of killing the goats never arose again.

Over time, they multiplied, and Leyla's parents realized that goat's milk was edible and even very tasty. They learned to make cheese and all sorts of goodies from the milk, and they became the wealthiest people in the area where they lived, and everyone around them came to them to learn their craft and to ask for goats to start their own herds. In exchange, they gave them what they had, so Leyla's family became the richest and happiest family thanks to Leyla's big heart.

And so, the wild goats became domesticated. Thus, Leyla's compassion and love for her animal friends not only enriched her family's life but also paved the way for a new era of prosperity and harmony in their community.

The characters and events may have been fictional, but the attitudes they displayed resonate in our society today and can spark intriguing discussions about who agrees or disagrees with them and why. The truths are as follows: 1. The climate is constantly changing, either gradually or abruptly, but always changing, just like the society we live in. 2. The progress of humanity is attributed not only to advancements in crafted objects but even more so to the transition from being hunter-gatherers to becoming plant cultivators and animal breeders. 3. The domestication of animals took place towards the end of the Stone Age, largely during the period known as the Neolithic.

Tariq and the Domestication of Sheep

IN THE GRAND NARRATIVE of humanity, one of the most significant chapters is that of animal domestication. This process not only radically altered the course of human life but also served as a turning point in our species' evolution. Just as we saw in Leyla's tale and her wonderful bond with the goat, this act of taming wild creatures marked a defining moment for humanity.

Like Leyla's story of goat domestication, which illustrated the profound connection between humans and nature, this tale of sheep domestication takes us back in time to the Stone Age, particularly to the late stages known as the Neolithic period. Thus, following this story, we will uncover not only a chronicle of the past but also a profound tribute to our close relationship with the animal world. If you recall, in the tale of goat domestication, the obstacle was Leyla's parents' desire to eat the goats, and it was only Leyla's big heart that spared their lives. In the story of sheep domestication, the major obstacle was their timid nature and their tendency to act solely as a flock, devoid of individual initiative.

Let's begin our story. Tariq was a 16-year-old boy who lived alone because his parents had passed away when he was still young. He lived in Northern Mesopotamia, in a fertile region crisscrossed by rivers like the Euphrates and the Tigris, which provided water for irrigation and agriculture. The vast plains were mainly cultivated for crops such as wheat and barley, and the climate was predominantly arid, with hot summers and milder winters.

Tariq's relatives were mainly involved in agriculture, and additionally, some of them developed pottery techniques and stone processing for construction and tools. The communities in this region where he lived were among the first to establish permanent settlements and develop primitive forms of social organization, but Tariq was poorer and lived from day to day. Not only was he poor, but many regarded him as somewhat odd, for he had the habit of wandering for hours on end, hands clasped behind his back, passing by people sometimes without even noticing them, lost in thought.

He had the habit of wandering everywhere, but he especially loved wooded areas where wild sheep and goats roamed. He always had a fondness for sheep, but they were so skittish that he could never get close enough to lay a hand on them. Yet he pondered much; at night, he dreamed of lambs, and by day, he schemed of ways to catch one. He attempted countless times to approach them with slow steps, but to no avail. Then he tried with movements so slow, yet even when he was a bit closer, in a second, they all fled from him.

One day, he had an idea he hadn't tried before, and it turned out to be brilliant. He went into the woods, and when he got as close to the herd of sheep as he could without them fleeing, he sat down on the ground and, in a soft voice, began to speak to them. He said all sorts of nonsense that came to his mind, and then he spoke to them as if he were talking to people, but always in a gentle tone. The impact on the sheep was immediate and immense.

They all stopped chewing and listened intently to Tariq's voice. Then, slowly but surely, a rather large and incredibly beautiful sheep began to approach him. It broke away from the group (which had never happened before, like a sheep breaking away from the group, especially when they identified a source of danger) and went to him. It looked long into Tariq's face, and he slowly raised his hand and stroked its head. After a while, the sheep returned to the group, and they all resumed chewing.

Tariq returned home very happy and slept until the next day, like a little child. The next day, he went to the sheep again, and the scene repeated itself exactly as the day before. Tariq got the sheep used to him every day by speaking to them kindly, sometimes feeding them by hand. Meanwhile, at home, he prepared a special place to keep them if he succeeded in bringing them home. And indeed, in the end, one by one, they allowed themselves to be tied to Tariq and taken home with him because they had come to trust him.

He became the happiest man of all and the first shepherd in that region. Now he could walk with the sheep from morning until evening; no one thought he was crazy anymore. Instead, many learned from him how to tend the sheep and what to do with their milk and wool. He encouraged them to treat the animals well, telling them that animals don't understand our facial expressions. It's useless to smile at them because they don't understand that we have good intentions towards them. Instead, if we speak to them gently, rarely, and in a soft voice, they will immediately understand what we want to tell them.

In the end, Tariq showed that true connection and understanding between humans and animals can be achieved through patience, kindness, and a gentle voice, reminding us that empathy and compassion can bridge even the widest gaps between species.

The events in the story are fiction, just like the character Tariq.

Historical truths are as follows: 1. The domestication of animals was a significant step in human history and the development of civilizations. 2. Sheep domestication likely first occurred in the Neolithic era in southern Anatolia, northern Mesopotamia, and Iran. 3. During the same period, other animals were also domesticated, including goats, the Auroch (ancestor of cattle), buffalo, gaur (wild ox), and pigs.

The Mammoth Hunting

ONCE I MENTION MAMMOTH, people will think of two things. That it's huge, which is true, and that it was hunted by humans in the Stone Age, which again is true. But not many ponder that not all mammoth hunts ended with the mammoths being killed; on the contrary, many times mammoths managed to kill their attackers, and many humans perished as a result. Today, I'll tell you about a fortunate case and, at the same time, the most amusing mammoth hunt in the history of the world! Let the adventure begin!

In the Stone Age, mammoth hunting was a challenging and perilous activity, but for many hunter-gatherer communities of that era, it represented a crucial source of food, fur, and other resources. Using rudimentary stone tools such as spears and arrows, ancient people hunted mammoths in groups, often employing elaborate techniques and strategies to catch and kill them.

One day, the tribe known at that time as the Mighty Bear Tribe gathered to discuss various important issues in the tribe's life, among them the news that a previously unknown mammoth had appeared nearby where they lived. A large specimen with dark brown fur. Someone from the tribe saw it and spread the news to others. Given the risks and difficulties involved in hunting such a large and powerful animal as the mammoth, it required a collective effort from many men.

First, they decided who would participate in the hunt. Small children, the elderly, the sick, and women were not allowed to go, everyone else wanted to go. Even though it was dangerous, it was also a great prestige, especially for the younger boys if they were finally considered old and capable enough to participate in a real mammoth hunt. The bigger or more dangerous the animal, the harder it is to bring it down, the greater honor the hunters gain, and, of course, more food for the tribe. They hunted mammoths for their meat and for fur, but most of all, they enjoyed the tusks, as they made the best tools out of them, and for the girls, they made jewelry.

After this meeting, where they discussed everything about the upcoming hunt, everyone went home, but in families, almost everyone continued the discussions about mammoths; they were so enthusiastic!

Zara is a lovely girl who has six older brothers. After six boys, a little girl was born. She was breathtakingly beautiful, but as she grew up among boys, she behaved like them, had activities like the boys, and did everything like them and together with them, but she was not allowed to go hunting and was saddened because of it.

-Boys, we're ready to hunt down that mammoth. Let's show everyone who the real hunters are in this family!

-Yeah, we're the best! We've grown up in these wild woods and learned all the secrets of hunting. Nothing can stop us!

-Exactly! The mammoth doesn't stand a chance against us. We'll show everyone how strong and brave we are!

-And when we bring it down, let's not forget to share the tusks. The girls will be thrilled to receive jewelry made by our skilled hands!

-Yes, and they'll surely be grateful for our gifts. Who wouldn't love jewelry made from tusks?

-We'll be honored throughout the village for what we've accomplished. We'll be elevated in everyone's eyes and proudly display our triumph! This is how all the men talked at home, boasting in front of their women, and some already imagined all sorts of stories, each more fantastic than the last, where they appeared as heroes, thinking that since the girls wouldn't be there and they would return with the prey, whatever story they told, the girls would believe. And they smiled as if they had already experienced those sweet moments. Meanwhile, Zara pondered how to seize a moment when she wouldn't be seen by her parents and secretly follow the boys to see what happened. She was curious and brave, but also quite mischievous.

The big day arrived. The boys and men set off for the hunt, and Zara, according to her plan, found a moment when her parents were not paying attention to her, and she ran after the hunters. No one saw her, but she followed them everywhere. At home, the women awaited the outcome of the hunt with great trepidation. They feared for the lives of the men, as many had perished in such hunts before, but they also eagerly anticipated the promised jewelry and all the treasures that followed a successful hunt.

At first, everything proceeded as usual. The boys found the mammoth, attacked it systematically, as they had planned, wounded it with many spears, and attempted to drive it towards a place where it could not escape and would be vulnerable. The forest echoed with the thunderous beat of drums as the hunters closed in on their prey. The shadows danced atop the trees, courtesy of the flickering torchlight, casting eerie lights on the tense faces of the men.

The mammoth, massive and imposing, trumpeted in defiance as the spears rained down upon its thick hide. With each strike, the hunters' cries mingled with the beast's roars, creating a cacophony of sound that reverberated through the night. The hunters' hearts raced as they lunged forward, their muscles straining with exertion. They moved with calculated precision, each maneuver bringing them closer to victory. With every step, hope surged within them, fueling their determination to bring down the mighty creature before them.

But the mammoth, undeterred by the onslaught, fought back with ferocious strength. Its tusks slashed through the air, sending shards of wood flying in all directions. The ground shook beneath its massive bulk as it charged forward, trampling everything in its path. Amidst the chaos, a sense of exhilaration swept over the hunters. They shouted with fervor, their voices rising above the din of battle. Victory seemed within their grasp, the culmination of weeks of preparation and anticipation. The animal, exhausted from so many arrows and blows, seemed to be nearing the end of its life, yet no one had the courage to approach close enough to deliver the fatal blow. Everyone wanted to be the one to kill it, but no one dared to get close. In the meantime, daylight had come. As the sun peeked over the horizon, the marshland seemed to come alive with the frantic energy of the trapped mammoth. With a sudden surge of strength, the mammoth hoisted its massive legs high into the air, defying gravity for a brief moment before crashing back down into the murky waters of the swamp.

In that instant, a torrent of mud erupted from the depths, showering the hunters from head to toe in a thick, slimy coating. The hunters, caught completely off guard, stared wide-eyed in disbelief, their mouths agape as they struggled to comprehend the absurdity of the situation.

But before they could even begin to process what had just happened, chaos ensued. With a collective shriek of terror, the hunters scattered in all directions, their panicked cries echoing through the forest as they fled for their lives. In stark contrast to the hunters' horror, Zara's clear voice suddenly rang out with laughter. Perched high in a tall tree, she witnessed the entire scene unfold. Descending from the tree, she raced home, still laughing heartily. She arrived ahead of the hunters, but soon they trickled in one by one, each of them exhausted and with shattered dreams, embarrassed by their own failure.

At home, Zara had already recounted the entire tale to the women and those who remained behind. She told them how the men had been instantly covered in mud, how terrified they had fled home, and how the mammoth had emerged from the swamp and gone on its way. The failed mammoth hunt left the tribe with muddy clothes and bruised egos, yet it also forged a bond of shared laughter and storytelling that would be retold with fondness for generations to come.

The characters and the story were fictional. Historical truths are as follows: In the Stone Age, humans hunted mammoths for their meat, fur, and tusks. Their excessive hunting may have contributed to the extinction of this species, along with other factors such as natural climate changes and competition with other species.

The Fire's Origin

ONCE UPON A TIME, LONG, long ago, in an era we now call the Stone Age, four people gathered around a fire to warm themselves. Grandfather Nok, his granddaughter Nika, and two of his friends. They discussed all sorts of important matters in the tribe's life when one of them said, "Oh, that was before the receiving of fire." Nika lifted her head and asked:

-What do you mean before the fire? But haven't we always had fire?

-No, my dear girl, when we were young, we didn't even know about the existence of fire, let alone how to make it! We ate everything raw, and often at night, animals would attack us, but now we can keep them at bay. It wasn't always like this.

-But when did you make the first fire?

-Just a little before you were born. But we didn't make it ourselves; we only received it from the tribe of the White Bears. Five people went after it!

-Why five?! It can't be that hard; could one person not bring it alone? How did it happen?

-It was a very big deal, a true miracle back then, and the tribe of the White Bears didn't want to give it to us. We offered them a lot of prey in exchange—wild boars, horses, all sorts of goodies—but they wouldn't give it to us.

-Why?

-They didn't tell us, but I think they didn't want us to be as strong as them. Fire had improved their lives so much that they believed if we were as strong and healthy as them, we would be a threat to them.

-And how did you finally convince them to give it?

-I don't remember anymore, or maybe I never knew.

-I know how—said Bram, one of the grandfather's friends. I heard that someone from our tribe realized that the chief of the White Bears tribe had a weakness for objects made of ivory, meaning he really liked them. So, the wealthy ones among us gathered, collected a chest full of beautiful objects, each more stunning than the last, and sent them to the chief of this tribe. He accepted the gift, and soon he showed kindness towards us and promised to give us a small fire.

-I hadn't heard of this, but if you say so, Bram, I believe you— said Grandfather.

-And how did they bring it? Why did five of them go after just one small fire?

-Because they were afraid it might go out on the way. They made five torches, as they had seen that tribe do, one for each, and they went to them. Only one of them went in to get the fire; they wouldn't have allowed more, and as soon as he got away from them enough so that no one from that tribe could see him, he lit the other four torches of the others. That way, slowly, they made their way home. When the wind blew out one person's fire, the others would light it again. And so, many times the torches went out before they reached home, but there was always one or two with the fire burning, and that's how they made it home safely. What a celebration it was then! It was unforgettable!!!

-How was it?

-Oh, the women and the whole village, from the youngest to the oldest, gathered and sang in honor of those who brought the fire! They brought branches and flowers, danced with joy, and everyone pushed to get the fire for themselves and their homes. The whole village was in a light, like the day when the sun shone.

-Yes, I remember that too! Poor Bunt's house even caught fire; no one knows to this day who set it, or perhaps it was an accident—added Bram.

-Yes, but the whole village helped him rebuild his house afterward, and in a few days, they were done—added Kroog.

-That's right.

-But where did they get the fire from? Who made the first fire? asked little Nika.

-No one knows that.

-But I do! I heard that one evening, the chief was arguing so loudly with his wife that their house's roof caught fire. Ha. ha. ha.

-Bram!!! Stop talking nonsense in front of the girl! scolded grandfather.

-But who made the first fire?!

-I don't know, my dear, but I heard a story that said a beautiful bird like you've never seen before, flew across the sky every evening, and the son of the chief of the White Bears tribe tried to hunt it, but he never succeeded in bringing it down. However, one day he managed to hit its tail, from where a feather as red as fire fell, which, when it reached the ground, lit some branches gathered near their house. That's where the fire came from, but that's just a story.

-Beautiful story, Gramps!.....Why don't you say anything, Mr. Kroog? Don't you know who made the first fire and how?

-No, I don't know either. And I only know one story, which I don't think is true.

-Please tell me!!

-The sun had a daughter as beautiful as him, named Beauty. He loved her more than anything else in the world. This girl looked down at us every day, watching how we lived, how we enjoyed ourselves, how we danced, smelled the flowers in the field, petted the animals, and laughed, but she loved the flute music the most. There was a young man who played the flute very beautifully, and she decided she wanted to learn to play the flute too and wanted to come down to earth. She begged her parents to let her. They didn't really want to, but she cried so much that they eventually allowed her.

She came down among us, and the sun always had his eyes on her. We could hardly sleep for a few hours, and it was day again, and what a day it was!!!! It was so hot that our round forest almost became a desert. It didn't rain anymore—no wind, no breeze, nothing! We were all dying of heat. Nobody knew how the girl was living, but one day she came among us and started singing to us. She learned to sing incredibly beautifully; she could do anything with the flute she wanted. She had beautiful melodies; she imitated the birds' songs; she almost didn't speak. And now, before me, the beautiful girl was holding the flute made from the cave bear's bone; it had maybe four or five holes, I don't remember. As she sang, some bad people gathered and decided to kidnap her. The sun, as he always had his eyes on her, got angry in a second; black cloud formed like the biggest rain we'd ever seen, and he struck lightning right in the middle of those bad people who wanted to kidnap the girl. Then everything around them caught fire, and that's how the first fire came to us.

-And those people died?

-Yes, they all died.

-And what happened to the girl?

-The Sun took her back with him, with the flute and everything, and more; I think they even took the young man from whom she learned to play, just to make sure the Sun that the girl wouldn't leave him again.

-How beautiful!!! That's the most beautiful story about fire!

-I'm glad you liked it!

And so, under the starlight of the fire, the story of the origin of fire intertwined with the memories and beliefs of the tribe, giving rise to many legends full of mystery and beauty. Each version brought to light brings with it a new understanding and appreciation for the power and miracle of fire, a symbol of warmth, protection, and community. In their hearts, these stories will always remain lit like living flames, reminding them that sometimes the origin of things can be as mysterious and wonderful as the flame that lights their way.

The characters and the story's action are fictional. The historical truths are as follows: The origin of fire is a complex and fascinating subject in human history. Generally, the exact process by which fire was discovered is not definitively known because it occurred in prehistoric times without written records. However, there are several theories and hypotheses regarding how early humans may have discovered and controlled fire:

Natural discovery: Some researchers believe fire was discovered accidentally when lightning struck a tree or dry vegetation, causing natural wildfires. Humans could have observed these fires and learned to control and utilize them for their own benefit.

Friction: Another theory suggests that humans discovered fire through friction by rubbing two dry materials together (such as wood or stones), generating enough heat to spark and ignite dry tinder.

Fire acquired from animals: There is also a hypothesis that humans may have observed wild animals using fire or acquired fire from them, for example, from lightning-induced fires or natural vegetation burns.

Systematic experimentation: Another scenario is that early humans systematically experimented with different materials and methods to produce fire until they discovered effective techniques for igniting and maintaining flames.

In conclusion, the exact origin of fire remains largely a mystery, but it is clear that the discovery and control of fire had a significant impact on human evolution, influencing technology, social behavior, and human lifestyle throughout history.

The Bone Flute

MANY, MANY YEARS AGO, during the era we now call the Paleolithic, a family lived in a small forest. There was a father, a mother, and two daughters: the older one and the younger one, named Nara. They lived very differently from how we live today, in a very simple hut they had recently moved into from a cave, as the cave had been too cold, dark, and damp. Although the cave had offered better protection from wild animals, the family decided to try this new type of dwelling they had seen others using at the time. They already knew how to make fire, and they felt much better now that they had left the dark cave.

Just as some people today are exceptionally skilled in music and dance, like the Romani people, who are unparalleled in these arts, there were families in the Paleolithic era renowned for their musical and dancing talents. Nara's family was one of these extraordinary families. Every member was exceptional, especially the men, who crafted all kinds of objects to produce loud, resonant sounds. They stretched animal hides and struck them with different sticks, creating various sizes of drums that produced different pitches.

But their most treasured instrument was a flute made by Nara's grandfather, discovered by Nara's father after the grandfather passed away. For a long time, it had not been played, as the grandfather had been ill towards the end of his life. Now, however, Nara's father gifted it to her, as he loved her dearly and had discovered her own musical talent. It was a marvelous instrument, crafted from the femur of a bear, with four holes, allowing it to produce not just a single note but multiple tones. Its voice was so sweet that it could melt even the heart of the cruelest person. Even the animals were fond of it when they heard Nara playing on it so beautifully. There was a fox who came near their house every evening just to listen to Nara play. Everyone said she had an enchanting flute, one that could tame even the wildest of creatures.

Nara was a brunette, with skin that was rather dark in color, and she had bright, shining eyes. She was very cherished by everyone, but her father loved her the most. One beautiful sunny day, after spending a long time indoors due to heavy rain, they decided to go out to gather mushrooms, as they often did. People in the Paleolithic era were much closer to nature than most of us are today; they knew very well which plants were edible and which were not, including mushrooms. They collected various types, with their father showing them what to pick and what to avoid.

What happened next, we do not know for certain, but what is clear is that after they returned home and cooked the mushrooms, they all ate and fell horribly ill. They had stomachaches and headaches; it was terrible. But what was even more tragic was that sweet Nara died then. Perhaps being the youngest in the family, her body couldn't withstand the poison of the mushrooms. You can imagine how devastated and sorrowful they all felt for her loss, especially her father, who mourned her deeply.

Her father blamed himself as if he had killed his own daughter because he was the one who showed them which mushrooms to pick and which to avoid. He felt profoundly guilty about her death, not just saddened by the loss. Although today we know that they might not have picked a poisonous mushroom at all, it's possible that a good mushroom was near a poisonous one, and with rain and wind, tiny parts of that poisonous mushroom could have ended up on the good one. So it's not out of the question that her father hadn't made any mistakes at all. Nevertheless, he was not only extremely saddened by his daughter's death, but he also felt guilty.

He stopped doing anything during the day and just cried, and at night he sighed in bed, staring longingly at the starry sky. That's what he did day after day, week after week, and month after month. He was no longer good for anything. He weakened, couldn't work, and didn't do anything, until a wonderful event happened that changed his life.

One night he dozed off a bit, but he didn't even know if it was true or a dream; he had the feeling as if it had happened in reality. Nara entered his room!!! She was wearing a white dress, with something resembling dove wings on her back and a crown of flowers in her hair. She looked at him and, in a calm voice, reprimanded her father, telling him not to cry for her anymore. "I am well; don't cry for me, but rejoice because I am happy! I see you every day, and it saddens me to see you crying. If you want to feel me closer to you, wake up at midnight and come to the garden; I'll sing for you!"

That was the entire dream, but when the father woke up, he was a different man. He felt such peace and joy as he had never felt in his life before! He got up, aired the room, washed his face, ate, and went to work. He chopped wood all day, far from everyone, without saying a word. He didn't want to lose that happy state of mind. Everyone was amazed at how much he had changed all of a sudden, and that evening he called his wife and other daughter and told them what he had seen last night, to console them as well, and assured them that Nara was somewhere living and happy.

Everyone rejoiced. There was only one thing he didn't tell anyone: that Nara had promised him that if he woke up at midnight and went to the garden, she would sing to him. He didn't tell anyone about that, but that's what he did. Every night he got up and went to the garden, sitting under a large tree, staring at the stars for hours. He then returned to his room and went to bed. No one knew why he did this, but since he worked during the day and was always cheerful, no one asked anymore.

Only he and the fox could hear Nara's singing at night; no one else could hear the beautiful music. But the whole community noticed that after that night, this father started playing instruments again, especially that flute, which had belonged first to his father and then to Nara, and everyone noticed that with each passing day, he played more and more beautiful melodies on it. They even dubbed it the enchanted flute.

As the days passed, the enchanting melodies of the flute filled the hearts of the villagers with joy and hope—a reminder of the enduring power of love and the resilience of the human spirit. And so, in the quiet of the night, under the watchful gaze of the stars, the legacy of Nara's music continued to echo through the ages, weaving its magic into the fabric of their lives, forever cherished and remembered.

This story was inspired by a true event, and we dedicate it to the people who inspired us with their stories. The prehistoric flute was found in 1951 in what is now Hungary, in a cave called Istállós-kői Cave.

Cave Paintings

CAVE PAINTINGS HAVE fascinated and intrigued people from their discovery to the present day. They are found on every continent, each reflecting the cultural specificities, environment, and era in which they were created. The most renowned among them, particularly for their artistic beauty, include the paintings in Lascaux and Chauvet Caves in France, Altamira Cave in Spain, and Coliboaia and Cuciulat Caves in Romania. They also provide us with information, or rather clues, about human evolution, daily life, and the religious and cultural beliefs of prehistoric people.

Today, I will share a funny story related to one of these caves, perhaps the most studied and well-known of them all, the Lascaux Cave in France. Once upon a time, there was a boy named Buru who loved to hunt bison and deer, and he especially enjoyed the taste of deer meat because he found it to be delicate and flavorful, with a slightly sweet taste and juicy texture. Almost every day, he went hunting.

Once, while wandering among hills and valleys and dense forests rich in wildlife and vegetation, he discovered a large cave, unknown to anyone from his tribe. He took with him two torches that shone brightly, and their fire was hard to extinguish, so he ventured into the cave. Being very curious, he wanted to explore the area. The cave turned out to be much larger and deeper than he expected, so he only went into a certain point, so as not to get lost and not be able to get out. But he advanced far enough to notice some interesting paintings on the walls—ones he had never seen or heard of before. He didn't have to walk far before noticing various animals painted on the cave walls: bison, deer, and other drawings he couldn't understand. Then, as he ventured further into the cave, he discovered many horses drawn on the walls. He had never seen anything like it before, but he immediately recognized the animals by their shapes painted on the walls.

His first thought was to run home and bring the whole tribe there to see what he had discovered. He set off quickly, already imagining how surprised the others would be, but when he reached the cave entrance, he changed his mind. A brilliant idea came to him, or so he believed it. He paused for a moment. He burst into laughter, then continued on his way home, smiling until he arrived. What was so funny? We'll find out soon.

He had a younger friend whom he asked to go through the entire tribe and inform all the men to come to him because he had something important to say, something they had never heard in their lives! This friend went, and by evening, most of them had gathered eagerly, coming to see what it was about and what was so important that Buru called the whole village together. They pondered various scenarios, some dark, some hopeful. Some of the people imagined that their homes were in danger; perhaps a rival tribe was planning something against them and Buru had found out; or maybe he had found wild horses somewhere and wanted to call them to catch the horses; everyone imagined something different.

When everyone had finally gathered, Buru spoke. With a solemn, serious, and majestic demeanor, he began to speak slowly, deliberately, and loudly:

-Fellow hunters and brothers! As we gather here tonight, under the vast expanse of the starlit sky, I come before you with a matter of great importance! Tonight, my brethren, I bring news that may shake the very foundations of our existence! It is a revelation that I have discovered in the depths of the earth. I found something that none of you has ever seen before, and you cannot even imagine such a thing! I found a bunch of bison, which are neither alive nor dead! Horses that are neither alive nor dead! Deer that are neither alive nor dead! Animals that run and, at the same time, stand still! You can't even imagine such things!!!!

-What do you mean they're neither alive nor dead??? And how can they run while standing still? everyone wondered.

Some believed, others didn't, they began to argue among themselves about whether such a thing was possible. Buru let them argue for a few moments, and then he spoke again.

-Quiet!! Make peace!! Whoever is interested and wants to see, come to my right. Those who are not interested should go home.

Slowly, everyone lined up to his right.

-Now, whoever wants me to show them the animals, bring me a deer or other prey you have hunted. As soon as you all bring me an animal, we can leave. Whoever brings me deer, I will show them many deer. Whoever brings me a bison, I will show them many bison. Whoever brings me a horse, I will show them many horses. You will surely be able to catch them. But I tell you, they are neither alive nor dead.

So, driven by the desire to win but especially by curiosity, everyone brought him an animal, whoever had one. When he gathered the animals from everyone, they set off on the road. The people's impatience reached its peak. They almost ran to the cave, barely speaking to each other, each eager to outpace the others. Some whispered jokes, but all in a hurry, the older ones struggling to keep up with the younger ones. When they reached the cave, they all entered in a heap. Buru showed them with a majestic tone:

-Look bison! Look, deer! Look, horses!

The people's amazement was immense. They touched the walls and the paintings; they had never seen anything like it! For a few moments, no one could speak from astonishment, but quickly their silence turned into the loudest screams! They became furious! They realized that these animals could not be hunted; they could not be eaten. They all screamed and ran to catch Buru—to kill him! To make him neither dead nor alive!

Buru, understanding that the situation was serious, started to run, the people after him! That's how they ran home, chasing Buru, but he managed to disappear among the trees, into the forest. He never returned to the village, but he managed to take with him some of the animals that were alive, which he received from the people in exchange for showing them the cave with the animals. It took a long time for the people to calm down. They were furious because they each lost an animal, and they couldn't even punish Buru as he deserved.

However, after many years, they remembered with amusement what had happened, and they named the cave "Buru's Cave". In the annals of time, the legend of Buru and the miraculous cave lived on, a testament to the enduring power of curiosity and the mysteries of our ancient past. And as the sun sets over the rugged landscape, casting its golden hues upon the forgotten caverns, we are reminded that some secrets are meant to be uncovered, while others remain shrouded in the mists of time, awaiting the curious souls who dare to seek them out.

The story of Buru and the characters are fictional. The historical realities are as follows:

1. Lascaux cave paintings offer a remarkable window into the prehistoric world, providing insights into the daily lives, beliefs, and artistic capabilities of humans in the Upper Paleolithic era.

2. Situated in the Dordogne region, the Lascaux cave is famous for the complexity and beauty of its paintings.

3. These paintings depict animals such as horses, bulls, bison, and deer.

4. Cave paintings provide clues about the religious and cultural beliefs of prehistoric people.

5. Prehistoric painters used natural pigments, such as red ochre, yellow ochre, and manganese black or charcoal, to create these images. Techniques include engraving the walls and applying pigment with brushes made from animal hair or by blowing pigment onto the cave wall.

6. It is believed that the paintings had a ritual or religious significance, possibly related to hunting or the fertility of animals.

7. The cave was discovered in 1940 by four teenagers accompanied by a dog. Due to damage caused by visitors, the original cave was closed to the public in 1963. To allow people to see and appreciate the cave art, detailed replicas of the cave were created, known as Lascaux II, III, and IV. Lascaux IV opened in 2016, offers an immersive and educational experience using state-of-the-art technology to reproduce the original cave as faithfully as possible.

The First Friend

ONCE UPON A TIME, THERE was a tribe renowned for its skilled hunters. They were numerous, numbering around 100–120 individuals, which was quite significant for that time. Other nearby tribes had far fewer people and were less organized. They hunted large herds of animals, not just individual prey. Of course, this required the cooperation of a larger group of hunters.

This tribe was also famous for its excellent tools crafted from flint and obsidian, materials from which they made knives, spearheads, scrapers, and chisels used for working wood, animal horn, and ivory. Although they had already begun cultivating certain plants, hunting and gathering remained important activities for procuring the necessary food.

In this tribe lived little Hanno, a handsome and clever boy who never managed to catch anything while hunting. Even in driving animals towards natural traps, such as precipices, ravines, or swampy areas, where animals were easier to kill, he was of no use, even though his father was a very skilled hunter. His father was indeed ashamed of him, but he still took him hunting, hoping for some miracle to happen and for him to catch something too. They also had some new weapons, a kind of bow that Hanno was quite skilled at shooting at home, but he never hit anything while hunting.

One day, a smaller but highly skilled group, armed with talent and weapons, went to hunt a herd of wild horses, with Hanno and his father joining them. Hanno was completely useless to the group, as usual, but he didn't feel sad about it at all. On the contrary, instead of hunting, he went to catch a little animal he had noticed in a bush, but not to kill it, but to take care of it. It was a small and adorable creature, but one that cried horribly. It was scared, hungry, and thirsty; it probably had fallen from somewhere and become separated from its mother.

It resembled a wolf cub, but it had more white on its face and chest than wolves usually have, and its legs, ears, and even around its eyes were white. It was very scared and wouldn't let itself be caught. But neither would Hanno give up until he caught it. Want to know how he caught it? He realized that the little one was extremely thirsty and gave it water right from his hands. At first, the little animal kept running away from him, but finally was persuaded by its own thirst and Hanno's gentle voice. And after drinking from his hand, it gained such courage that it let itself be caught. Hanno picked it up and happily carried it to show his father.

His father was upset for a few moments, but when he heard the other hunters laughing at his son, he changed his attitude. He picked up the little animal, took his son by the hand with the other, and with determined steps and a strong voice, he walked into the midst of the hunters and said:

-This animal is ours now. Anyone who dares to harm it or mock my son will have to deal with me! You'll have to fight me!

And so they returned home from the hunt without catching anything except the wolf pup. The other hunters laughed at them, saying, What kind of son does he have that never catches anything to eat, only a sick and hungry wolf pup? But they ignored them. They kept the pup, gave it food and water as needed, and it always wanted to be with Hanno. It stayed with him all day and slept with him at night. They lived in a dugout arranged in a natural oval-shaped pit, covered with animal skins, with a fire pit in the middle. This was where the wolf pup, whom they had named Blaze, loved to stay the most. Even after he recovered and they set him free, he didn't want to leave them.

With Blaze leading the way, he also brought his friends, who were delighted by the wonderful smells and the food they received from humans without having to catch anything for themselves, and the humans were pleased because they felt protected by their new friends from the attacks of other wild animals. As the sun dipped below the horizon, painting the sky in hues of orange and gold, Hanno and Blaze sat together, their unwavering friendship evident.

Through trials and triumphs, they had stood by each other's sides, becoming inseparable companions. In the quiet moments of dusk, they shared a knowing glance, understanding that they were more than just friends—they were each other's first friends. With hearts full of warmth and gratitude, they embraced the coming night, ready to face whatever adventures lay ahead, forever bound as The First Friend.

The characters and the story are fictional. Historical truths are as follows: The most important aspect of dog domestication lies in the profound bond formed between humans and canines over millennia. Through a process of mutual adaptation and interaction, dogs evolved from wild wolves into loyal companions, offering invaluable assistance in various tasks such as hunting, herding, and guarding. This domestication process highlights the remarkable ability of both humans and dogs to communicate, cooperate, and form enduring partnerships. Furthermore, the transformation of wolves into dogs exemplifies the power of selective breeding and the profound impact of human influence on the evolution of other species. Ultimately, the domestication of dogs represents a testament to the enduring connection between humans and animals, shaping not only our shared history but also our contemporary lives in profound ways.

Stone Age Beats

LONG AGO, TOWARDS THE end of the Stone Age, in a region of North Africa, there lived two rival tribes. There was not a significant difference between them, but they were always in competition with each other. The Garam tribe was slightly wealthier than the other tribe, Targa, and had a few more people in their community than the Targa tribe. In the Garam tribe, there were around 100 individuals, while in the Targa tribe, there were about 70. At that time, each tribe held most of their goods in common, and people had very few personal possessions. Although there was rivalry among individuals within each tribe, the rivalry between the tribes was even greater. Both tribes were engaged in hunting and gathering, but they also kept animals. Especially goats, but the Garam tribe also had a few pigs and cultivated slightly more grain than the Targa tribe.

The tribes lived quite close to each other. Taru was a clever boy who lived with the Targa tribe. His parents were quite respected in the tribe because they were skilled, especially in grain cultivation. Whenever the tribe gathered to decide something related to community life, they always took into account the opinions of Taru's parents.

What I haven't told you yet is that they were respected not only for their skill but also for their beautiful boy, who had a talent, if we can call it that. He liked to run through the village sometimes, to jump up, like small children do when they are happy, and to the rhythmic sound his feet made, especially if he did it somewhere on a ground that resonated well, to those sounds he danced. Sometimes he even sang, and as he grew a little, he made all kinds of drums with which he beat the rhythm.

He used wood to build the bodies of the drums, cutting different shapes and sizes to produce different sounds. Then he stretched goat skin over the wooden frame to form the striking surface, using plant fibers to fasten the skin to the frame. And the drums that turned out the best, whose sound he liked, he painted red and black, as he liked. But what made him even more special was that every time he sang and danced loudly, the rain would come. People liked this because it didn't rain very often for them, and they needed rain a lot. So as soon as they noticed this, that after he danced, the rain came, they liked him even more.

One day, the tribe held a gathering because they needed to decide on an important issue for everyone. Their problem was that a large herd of gazelles had appeared nearby, and they felt that the rival tribe was hunting many more gazelles than they were, and in general, they were wealthier than them. Which was true. And what some in the tribe thought to do was set fire to the houses of the rival tribe!! Some agreed, others didn't, but it seemed like the voice of those who agreed was stronger. However, Taru disagreed. He got really upset, and he tried to convince the others not to do such a thing.

-How could such a thing cross your mind? Do you realize what you're saying? To set fire to the entire Garam tribe? What are they guilty of? Do you realize that their children, the elderly, and their animals will suffer? What are they guilty of? That they are better hunters than us? It would be better for us to craft improved tools with which to hunt more easily. Or to choose from our tribe those who are best at hunting and have them teach us all how to hunt! Or if we can cultivate more grain and keep more animals, then we won't need so many gazelles. Or we can all move a little further away, where there is plenty to hunt. Do you realize that if we set fire to the Garam tribe, people could die?

-And what if they die? We'll have more food left. And those who don't die will have to rebuild their huts; it will take them some time to rebuild them, and they won't have as much time for hunting, at least until we hunt down this herd of gazelles. And in the end, whose side are you on? Aren't you from our tribe? Go and stay with them if you side with them more than with us!

That's what they told Taru, and they continued discussing all the details of how to set fire to the neighboring tribe. Taru didn't even stay for these discussions; feeling saddened, he left them and went home. As they agreed, so did the people of the Targa tribe. The next night, all the homes of the Garam tribe were engulfed in flames. No one saw them set the fire, but it was very clear to everyone that the Targa tribe was guilty, and it wasn't an accidental fire because all the homes caught fire almost at the same time. The poor people didn't even have time to put out the fire at one home before the next one was already burning. The entire village burned to the ground. You can imagine how much suffering was experienced!

Fortunately, no lives were lost in the fire, but quite a few animals died, and the ones that didn't die ran away wherever they could; none remained. It was an immense tragedy. It took the people of the Garam tribe quite some time to rebuild everything, and since they lost the animals they kept, they were forced to hunt even more. So the whole action was in vain for the Targa tribe, as the gazelles remained even fewer than if they hadn't set fire to the neighboring tribe.

However, they were punished even more severely for their deeds. Since that day, it hasn't rained on the Targa tribe. Not at all. Plants began to wither; they had nothing to feed the animals, and the springs ceased to flow. They didn't know what to do. They went to Taru to beg him to sing and dance as he used to, but he categorically refused.

They held a gathering, and they all begged Taru to dance, but he told them that he would only dance if they all went to the Garam tribe, took animals as gifts, and asked for forgiveness for what they had done. They thought about it a lot, but their shame was even greater than their thirst; they didn't accept it. How could they tell them that they had set fire to their homes? Although everyone already knew that.

Days passed, and still no rain. But it hadn't rained on the Garam tribe either. One day, an idea came to Taru: he took all his drums and went to the Garam tribe. He told them that he had come to sing and dance for them. They were overjoyed because they knew that if he danced, the rain would come, and after the disaster of the fire, they didn't need a drought either; they warmly welcomed him. Taru immediately started to dance, and within moments, it started to rain. But only for them. It was as if the sky had a curtain between the two tribes; it rained at Garam, and at Targa tribe, it was sunny.

Those from Targa were almost dying of envy and malice when they saw how well it was raining at Garam, but they didn't dare go to collect water because they had no right to be on another tribe's territory; it was guarded, and if anyone went there, they would be kicked out. After it rained enough, Taru returned home, but he still refused to dance at home. Every time there was a need at Garam, he took his drums and went to dance there, not at home. The people from the Targa tribe were furious with him, but no one dared to harm him. Every day, they tried to persuade him to dance for them, but he said that if they had ignored him twice, he wouldn't entertain their request now.

He suggested they go to the neighboring tribe and ask for water. Initially resistant, hunger and thirst eventually forced them to seek water from the rival tribe. Water was given, but only in exchange for animals. So, gradually, they traded one or two animals each day for water until they had none left. By then, Taru had danced for the Garam tribe until his tribe was bereft of a single animal.

This was a lesson that wrongdoing comes back to haunt you. The Taram tribe became even poorer, and the difference between the two tribes was now even greater, but the people understood their mistake and didn't repeat it, and over time, they became richer and better than they were before.

During the Stone Age, musical instruments were essential to the lives of early human communities, bringing sound and rhythm into a world filled with mystery and danger. These instruments were simple and rudimentary, yet highly valuable to their culture. Among them were bone flutes, which produced melodious tones through finger holes, and horn trumpets made from animal horns, used for rituals and communication through powerful sounds. Leather drums, stretched over wooden or bone frames, added rhythm and pulse to ceremonies and dances played with hands or sticks. Rattles, made from natural materials like shells, dried seeds, or small stones in natural shells, offered rhythmic sounds through simple shaking. Other percussion instruments, such as sticks and stones struck together, added texture and depth to their musical experiences.

The Fox's Treasure

ONCE UPON A TIME, IN an era we now call the Stone Age, the valley between the Tigris and Euphrates was known for its extensive marshlands and lakes formed by the rivers' overflows. These wetlands were home to a variety of plant and animal species, and here lived little Suri. She was a clever and pretty young fox. The tips of her ears were dark, almost black, as were her paws, while her belly and the tip of her tail were white. She liked to roam around human dwellings at night because she often found food there, though she was frequently chased away by dogs.

One night, while she was wandering as usual among the houses, she heard some people talking loudly by a fire. At first, she was more interested in the bones they occasionally tossed away after finishing their meal, but their conversation suddenly became interesting to her as well.

One of the men recounted that he had heard somewhere that in the middle of the lake lived a large pike, with a golden belly, and whoever managed to catch it, the pike would grant them three wishes. The discussion ignited; some believed it, while others did not. Some argued that the pike was a freshwater fish, preferring lakes, rivers, and marshes with cold and clear water, unlike the warm and sometimes arid regions where they lived. Others countered, saying that if the pike could grant any wish, why couldn't it live among them?

In any case, little Sura's imagination immediately embarked on an adventure-filled journey. She imagined how she would catch the pike, but she wasn't sure exactly what to ask of it. Sometimes she wanted one thing, sometimes another; it was hard for her to decide. She paid no attention to the voices saying that it was hard to catch because it slipped from one's grasp; she thought that clumsy humans might find it difficult, but with her fox claws, she would catch it immediately. She just didn't know how to get to the middle of the lake, where the magical pike was said to live.

She spent a night pondering what to ask of the pike if she caught it. She decided that her first wish would be for her den to always be filled with food, both for her and for all the foxes in the world, so that they would never go hungry again. Her second request would be to turn herself as white as snow. When she was very young, she had heard somewhere about a beautiful fox, white all over, and ever since then, she had wanted to become white too. And her third wish would be for all foxes to become immortal.

Once she had decided what to ask for, she went to the lake. She dipped a toe in the water, but it was as cold as ice, and she didn't like it at all, and she didn't even know how to swim. She hadn't thought about that. She was so excited to catch the pike with the golden belly that she hadn't even thought about how she would get to the middle of the lake. But being clever, she quickly figured it out. She grabbed a large log, lay on her belly on it, and paddled with her four paws until she reached the middle of the lake. What's more, she tied a piece of meat she had found along the way to her tail, and she planned to use that meat to catch the pike. She sat there in the middle of the lake, with her tail dipped in the water, but the pike didn't appear. She got bored and remembered that people said the pike not only lived in the middle of the lake but also very deep, somewhere at the bottom of the lake. So that was probably the problem; her tail didn't reach the bottom of the lake. So she returned to the shore, and once again, she pondered what to do.

As she stood there at the edge of the lake, she noticed that the people had begun to speak loudly, to argue, and she could see that the rain was coming. She already knew from experience that when people spoke loudly amongst themselves, and especially when rain was approaching, they weren't paying much attention to foxes, and before long, they would disappear into their homes. She knew that before rain, some fish were much easier to catch, because before a storm, the sky darkened, making the fish feel safer and less exposed to predators, and with the rising water level, they approached the shores more, to take advantage of the increased water level and the new food resources brought by the rain. Did humans not know this? Maybe they did, maybe they didn't; they didn't really like to fish in such weather, and they left their boats tied to the lakeshore.

That's all little Suri needed. She untied a boat, climbed inside, and found all the fishing gear there. No one noticed the boat drifting away from the shore. Suri hadn't even reached the middle of the lake, and she had already caught a very big fish! And not just any fish, but the magical pike!! She could hardly believe it! She barely managed to tell the pike her first wish. The pike granted it immediately, filling all the fox dens with food, only Suri couldn't see that from there in the middle of the lake. So she asked the pike:

—How can I know that you granted my first wish? Show me the dens filled with food, or else I won't believe you!

—Very well, Suri, I'll show you, but that was your second wish. There's only one more.

And just like that, she was instantly taken to the fox dens, which were indeed full. Suri was happy, but she regretted losing one wish out of three, which could have been granted if she hadn't been so distrustful. Now what to do? She pondered what to ask for. Should she become as white as snow, so that everyone will admire her beauty, or should she ask for immortality? She didn't want to give up either one. As she kept thinking and time passed, suddenly she saw that the pike was beginning to die because they were on dry land, and the pike couldn't live long without water, just a few moments. Suri was terribly frightened and began to scream.

—Please, pike, don't die! Don't die, pike, I beg you, don't die!

As soon as the pike heard this, it immediately turned back into the lake, but all it said to Suri was:

—Alright, Suri, I won't die, but that was your third wish.

To Suri's amazement, she didn't even know what to say or think. Even now, she couldn't believe that she had caught the magical pike, that it had granted her a wish. She felt sorry for losing two of the wishes she had initially planned to ask the pike for, but the joy of the other foxes, who didn't know about Suri's three wishes but suddenly found their dens filled with food that never ran out, this joy comforted Suri. She didn't think about what else she could have gained; she only thought about what she had gained. And the pike, who didn't tell Suri, but appreciated Suri's good intentions it felt sorry for him and thought more about not dying, and not about his third wish, without Suri knowing, gave him another gift. From that day on, people never killed any foxes; they didn't chase them away or hunt them for their fur. Over time, the foxes noticed, that everywhere foxes had problems with people, only they lived in harmony with people, but no one knew that this was also thanks to Suri, not even she knew. And so the foxes remained russet, with black ears and paws, instead of being as white as snow.

In conclusion, Suri's encounter with the magical pike not only granted her unexpected gifts but also brought about unforeseen harmony between foxes and humans. Despite losing two of her wishes, Suri found solace in the joy of her fellow foxes and the newfound peaceful coexistence with humans. As the russet foxes continued to roam the land, their once-black ears and paws became symbols of a hidden bond forged by one clever and compassionate fox named Suri.

The characters and the story are fictional, but their attitudes resonate among us in our society. Historical truths are as follows: The Fertile Crescent is a historical region located in the Middle East, renowned for its fertile soils and for being the cradle of several important ancient civilizations. It was the birthplace of agriculture and some of the earliest human civilizations, including the Sumerians, Akkadians, Babylonians, and Assyrians.

Foxes lived and still live in the Fertile Crescent region. Species such as the red fox (Vulpes vulpes) and the Rüppell's fox (Vulpes Rueppellii) are native to this region. These foxes are adaptable and can thrive in diverse habitats, including the semi-arid and desert regions of the Fertile Crescent. However, it is highly unlikely that pike and foxes would have coexisted commonly in the same region during the Paleolithic era due to significant differences in habitat and ecological needs.

The northern pike (Esox lucius), known as the pike, is a freshwater fish that prefers colder waters, typical of lakes and rivers in the northern regions of the northern hemisphere. In the Fertile Crescent, which includes regions in the Middle East (such as Iraq, Syria, Lebanon, Israel, and parts of Turkey), pike are not native. The climate and types of aquatic habitats in this area are not suitable for pike. In conclusion, while the story may be a work of fiction, it serves as a reminder of the enduring parallels between human nature and the natural world, offering insights into our shared past and the diverse ecosystems that have shaped our history and continue to influence our lives today.

The Precious Necklace

IN A TIME LONG PAST, during the Stone Age, there lived a tribe known as the Brave of the Forest. They were named so because they were indeed braver compared to other tribes, but they were renowned for another thing: they knew how to craft jewelry like no one else could. They mainly made necklaces, bracelets, pendants, and amulets from various materials, worn by both women and men. The women's jewelry differed slightly from what the men wore; however, it was often richer, more decorative than the men's, and made from less durable, more delicate materials such as shells and fine bones. The men's ornaments were somewhat simpler, meant to reflect their status as warriors or hunters, and the materials used were intended to command respect.

The precious necklace I will tell you about today was such a necklace that commanded respect from anyone who wore it. That's why the people of the tribe took great care of it, and it was passed down from father to son. It belonged to a family skilled in crafting beautiful jewelry, and this necklace was the most special of all they had ever made. It was finely crafted, but not overly decorative. It was made from pieces of marble, which were carefully perforated and polished, but it also had deer antlers among the marble beads and teeth from other animals living in the area.

But besides the necklace's beauty, it had another magical power: anyone who wore it not only gained respect from others but also never came to harm if they ever fought with people from another tribe, and during hunting, they were never killed or injured by animals, as often happened during those times. That's why this necklace was mainly worn by men, who took great care of it.

It was usually worn by the eldest son in the family, the one who hunted the most, and in the evening, it was placed in a specially crafted ceramic vessel made just for this necklace, so that during sleep, no deer antler or marble bead would break, and anyway, it wasn't a comfortable necklace to sleep with. In one fateful night, this enchanted necklace vanished. No one saw it, no one knew anything about it. A great commotion erupted among the people, suspicions shifting from one to another as they searched high and low, scouring every dwelling in the tribe, but to no avail. The eldest boy, who had last worn it, was devastated beyond words. He knew for certain he had placed it beside him as he slept in the ceramic vessel, yet come morning, it was nowhere to be found.

How could he not have awakened when the necklace was taken? He never slept deeply; it was his habit to stir at the slightest noise. He couldn't fathom how such a thing could have happened. Day and night, he thought only of the necklace, until even at night he dreamed of it. One night, he dreamed that a giant bear had stolen the necklace from him. As soon as he woke up in the morning, he went into the forest to search for the necklace. The forest was dense and frightening; here he had to face the dangers of nature, encounter wolves, and be attacked by a bear, but he escaped with his life, yet the necklace was nowhere to be found.

On another night, he dreamed that the necklace was in a deep cave. When he woke up, he took a torch and went to the nearby caves in search of the necklace. It was even more terrifying here; he was alone, and the caves were immense, with all sorts of unexpected challenges. Sometimes his torch went out, sometimes he didn't know how to find his way out of the cave, and sometimes he heard terrifying noises from animals he had no idea about. All the horror stories he had heard in childhood about evil spirits that wanted to kill people who entered caves came to his mind, so it was a frightening experience, and only his courage helped him not to die of fear there. However, he didn't find the necklace there either.

On another night, he dreamed that the necklace was underwater, somewhere on the edge of the lake but in the water. The boy, as soon as he woke up, ran to the lake, threw himself into the water, which was as cold as ice, and started swimming all along the edge of the lake. The lake was large, and he had a lot of swimming to do to check the entire shore of the lake, all around. But he did it. He came out of the water from time to time to warm up a little in the sun, then he went back. By evening, he had finished checking the entire shoreline of the lake, but the necklace was not there either.

On another night, he dreamed that his necklace was in a ruined, abandoned dwelling located on the territory of a rival tribe. He knew the place well, but it was dangerous to enter without being invited by someone; they could even kill him, thinking he had malicious intentions. Nevertheless, he went there to search for his lost necklace. He didn't go there during the day, but at night, to avoid being seen by anyone. He was clever; he managed to check the place without being seen, but on his way home, he was attacked by a pack of wolves. They surrounded him; there were about 15-20 wolves, and they growled horribly at him. There was one that approached him more than the others, ready to bite him, and it was just a matter of time before they all jumped on him. But he was smart; he knew that if 20 wolves jumped on him, he wouldn't stand a chance of surviving. Luckily, he had a stick with him. But with that stick, he didn't hit the wolves; if he had hit one, they would all jump on him. Instead, he spun it around him to keep them at a certain distance, slowly, with calm movements, and he began to speak to them in a soft voice. He talked and talked, and talked. It didn't matter what he said, just to convey to the wolves a sense of calm. And that's how it was; the wolves seemed hypnotized by his gentle voice, they calmed down, and slowly they moved away one by one from him, and he continued his journey home.

The boy returned home completely exhausted. He went to bed, and again he dreamed of the enchanted necklace. This time he dreamed it was at the top of a gigantic tree, one that would take a person three days to climb, like in fairy tales, or as tall as a baobab tree. But in the morning, to his family's surprise, he didn't go anywhere. When they asked him what he dreamed and why he wasn't going to search for the necklace, he replied that he had been deceived by his dreams four times and that he would never believe in dreams again as long as he lived. Dreams are dreams, and reality is reality.

And so, he went outside, whistling, and wandered wherever his feet took him. He needed a day of rest after so many failed attempts to find the enchanted necklace. The boy wandered into a breathtaking meadow, blanketed with vibrant wildflowers in every color imaginable. The air was filled with the sweet fragrance of blossoms, and butterflies danced gracefully from flower to flower. The gentle rustling of leaves and the distant song of birds created a serene and enchanting atmosphere.

He sat down on a large stone and suddenly heard an interesting conversation in the distance. A thin, chirping voice was trying to convince a fuller, more resonant voice to accept a beautiful and unique gift. The thin voice was telling its friend that it had brought the most beautiful adornment ever seen, a necklace made of imperishable seeds, and was trying to persuade the other that whoever wore that necklace would become the most handsome elephant in the world. Meanwhile, the boy slowly walked towards the place from where the sounds were coming. I think you've guessed which necklace of imperishable seeds the thin voice was talking about.

Reaching the spot, the boy witnessed an emotional scene: a small bird was just giving the magical necklace as a gift to a young elephant, who in turn was about to give the bird a heart he had made from a large red leaf, tied with a long, beautiful, velvet-like ribbon. Both, were happy, when they noticed the boy and started a conversation with him, unaware of the whole story of the necklace, that it belonged to the boy. They were so cheerful that they told the boy their whole life story. The young elephant and the bird had been friends for some time and had decided to celebrate their friendship. Each tried to give the other the most beautiful thing they could, with the bird believing that the most beautiful thing was the necklace made of seeds that never spoil, as a symbol of their eternal friendly love.

What could the boy tell them? Ruin their joy? He didn't say anything, went back home, and went to bed without telling anyone. That night, however, he had a beautiful dream. A beautiful girl appeared in his dream and said to him:

"Don't be sad anymore about the necklace. That necklace was made to protect you from wild animals, to make you strong and perseverant in your work and battles. So that no one could defeat you, to be wise and good. You lost this necklace, but in searching for it, you became brave, strong, perseverant, and wise. You learned not to believe in your dreams and became good. What more could you want? Now, without the necklace, you know everything, and no one can ever take your skill away. Cheer up and don't think about the necklace anymore!"

When he woke up in the morning, he was the happiest boy in the whole village. No one knew why, but from that day on, he had a joy like no one else in their village.

If anyone ever asked him about dreams, he would always tell them not to believe in dreams. However, if a dream brings great peace to the soul, that dream should not be forgotten. He would say no more. Besides virtues, he also gained the friendship of an innocent little bird, who had no idea the enchanted necklace belonged to someone, and the friendship of a sweet elephant, with whom he often met afterward since they lived nearby. In the end, the boy's life was richer and fuller because of the lessons he learned and the friends he made along the way. The enchanted necklace, now a symbol of his journey, remained a cherished memory. He lived happily, sharing his wisdom and joy with his tribe, forever changed by his adventures.

The story and characters are fictional, historical truths are as follows: In the Stone Age, people crafted ornaments from various materials such as stone, marble, shells, bones, animal teeth, and even metals in the later stages of the era. Ornaments were worn by both women and men, often with women's being more decorative. Wearing jewelry often had symbolic, spiritual, or social status significance, and it was a common practice in many prehistoric cultures.

The Clay Sentinel

ONCE UPON A TIME, IN the age we now call the Stone Age, there was a magical clay pot. Why do I say it was magical? It had a unique characteristic that no other clay pot ever had: it could speak both the language of humans and the language of animals. Because of this unique quality, it was very conceited. Let me describe how it looked: it was small and very plump, brown in color, with spots painted in red and yellow, and decorated with incised lines all over its body. Long ago, it had been handmade from a fairly fine material and fired in a kiln that was heated to very high temperatures to ensure the clay was well-baked. It was proud not only of its ability to speak but also because it had a human face. It had the face of a young lady, with thin lips and tiny, line-like eyes. Even though people had already discovered the potter's wheel by that time and greatly appreciated this new technology for making ceramic vessels, the young lady with thin lips was still very pleased with herself and believed she was the most beautiful clay pot on earth.

She refused to be used by humans. When they approached her, she would either give them a scornful look that frightened them or say something awful that scared them even more, and no one dared to touch her. She amused herself by frightening them and laughing so hard that her laughter could be heard by the neighboring tribe.

But she had another bad habit that tormented the people: when guests came to the family who owned her, she would start cursing and criticizing the guests, but she wouldn't open her eyes so no one would notice she was speaking. She would say all sorts of insults, calling them stupid, fat, or ugly. The poor hosts were so embarrassed they wished they could sink into the ground. After a while, no one wanted to visit them anymore. And because they were superstitious and afraid of the young lady with thin lips, their clay pot, they didn't dare throw her away. She laughed at them, her voice echoing to the neighboring village.

One day, the young lady felt bored. Naturally, she was bored, because she didn't allow people to put water in her, store grains, or even touch her. It's no wonder she got bored. And what do you think she decided to do? She decided to go for a walk. Being plump and round, she easily rolled out of the house, and since she was well-fired, she was sturdy and didn't break along the way. If she hadn't been fired at such a high temperature, she surely would have shattered on the road. But since she was made with great care and skill, she didn't break. This was yet another reason for her to be even more proud, and she thought to herself about the other clay pots she knew that hadn't been fired as well as she was, imagining how they would have broken on the same paths she traveled.

So, she rolled across green fields, filled with wonderfully fragrant flowers, listening to the birds chirping. But by the afternoon, clouds began to gather, and rain approached. Knowing she was well-fired, she eagerly awaited the rain, ready to show the world that she wasn't afraid of water, as she wouldn't dissolve or deform in the moisture, unlike ordinary clay pots. And so it happened. The rain came, but she wasn't afraid. She stood in the rain all night, and the next morning, when the sun rose, she dried out and looked even better than when she was first made.

She became even more proud. Thinking that since she was so special, she needed to find someone to serve her. And so, she headed into the forest to look for servants. But what happened there? You'll see it shortly. As soon as she entered the forest, she encountered a small, cute deer. Being so conceited, she wondered if she should accept such a servant, so small and ugly—at least that's how she perceived the deer, though it was not ugly at all, quite the opposite. While she was still thinking about whether to accept her as a servant or not, the deer greeted her!

–Good day, clay pot! What are you doing here in the forest? I've never seen a clay pot in the forest, only in people's houses. And how come you have a human face? Can you talk?

–Of course, I can talk! I know everything better than humans; I'm smarter and more beautiful than any of them, and besides, I'm immortal, unlike them.

–And why have you come here to the forest?

asked the deer.

–To avoid being bored with them. They are so dull, ugly, and stupid, and lately, since they started cultivating grains, they've become fat too... I can't stand them anymore.

The deer was surprised by such a response and asked further,

–Have you ever looked into the mirror of water? Have you seen what you look like?

–What do you mean, what do I look like? I'm the most beautiful in the world, small and delicate, with eyes like stars, lips like field flowers, and decorated with fine lines... in two words, most beautiful.

When the deer heard this, she laughed and said,

–To me, you look small and fat, just like you say the humans who bored you are. You have a huge belly, a very thick neck, black spots that don't suit you at all, a too-sharp nose, small eyes, and what else can I say? You think you're the most beautiful on earth?

And she laughed at her even more.

The clay pot, not used to such words and being exceedingly conceited, got so angry that she cracked on the spot and shattered into countless pieces. And so, in pieces, she lay there for hundreds and hundreds, thousands of years. Over time, she was covered by dust, by soil, and ended up deep in the ground.

Until one day, a team of archaeologists found her during an excavation. They reconstructed her because they also thought she was beautiful, placed her in a museum display, and hundreds and hundreds of people admired her. But she learned from what had happened; she never criticized anyone again, but neither did she speak anymore. Today, you can see many pots with faces in museums; which one is the talking one? I don't know, maybe you will find her and ask her how she is doing.

The characters and events in this story are fictional. The historical truths are as follows:

Face pots, also known as "anthropomorphic vessels," are ceramic artifacts dating back to the Neolithic period, characterized by the representation of human faces on their surfaces. These vessels have been found in various regions of the world and likely had multiple uses. They may have been used to store food, water, or other valuable goods. Another explanation is that the human faces on these pots could be linked to the religious practices and spiritual rituals of Neolithic communities; they might represent deities, ancestors, or protective spirits. Additionally, some face pots have been found in graves, suggesting they could have played a role in funerary rituals, perhaps as cult objects accompanying the deceased into the afterlife.

Lily the Clay Wonder

DID YOU KNOW THAT THE discovery of pottery dates back a considerable amount of time and that clay vessels, being harder to transport, are specific to sedentary communities? The oldest clay vessels in the world were found in Japan, belonging to the Jomon culture. Pottery was then independently discovered in other parts of the world. It appeared in the settlements of the Sahara oases, then in the Fertile Crescent and southern Anatolia, and spread to the Balkans and further south, reaching Ethiopia. But pottery also appears in India and on the American continent. Initially, pottery did not require any specialization; anyone could shape a vessel to be fired in an open flame. The major change, however, occurred with the discovery of the potter's wheel and kilns for firing pottery, which could reach very high temperatures, up to 800 degrees Celsius. Moreover, the construction of vaulted kilns allowed for even higher temperatures, exceeding 1000 degrees Celsius.

Lily, the little girl I want to tell you about today, once found a small statuette while playing in the field. It was about as long as a finger and as thick as two or three fingers. It was made of clay and fired but probably not at very high temperatures. Excited, she took it home. Her parents looked at the statuette but didn't know what it represented. It resembled a bird with a sharp beak, but it also seemed to have two human-like arms. The neighbors said it looked like a goat without horns. No one was particularly fond of the statuette, but Lily liked it. She placed it by her bed, and every night before falling asleep, she would look at it. To her, it seemed to represent a loving mother protecting her little girl.

One evening, as she was getting ready for bed and staring intently at the statuette, as she usually did, a strong wind suddenly blew through the room, and in an instant, she was transported to a beautiful field like she had never seen before, filled with flowers. These flowers were much more colorful and fragrant than the ones they had at home. But what surprised her even more was that when she touched her head, she noticed she had grown a hat, like a mushroom! Indeed, she looked like a mushroom with a red cap and white spots, and she was suddenly wearing a purple dress with white spots on it, just like the hat. Around her neck was green. And she wasn't alone; she saw a little girl smiling at her who looked just like her—a friendly little mushroom girl. What they talked about, I don't know, but they quickly became friends and began to roam the forest and field together, playing a lot. They could do this because not only did they have legs and could walk, but they were little mushrooms that could also fly and walk on the treetops if they wanted.

When it was a night at Lily's home, it was day there. So, her first night was her first day spent in the mushroom world. This entire world was inside the statuette she had found and looked at every day at home. When it got dark there, Lily had to go home so her parents wouldn't notice her absence; this enchanted world was accessible to her only if she didn't tell anyone about it. When she was ready to leave, the wind would come and take her back home to her bed. Lily spent many nights, or rather many days, in great joy without telling anyone about the enchanted world of the mushrooms.

Then one day, something terrible happened. She and her mushroom friend went into the forest, where they had been many times and knew the place well, but they got lost. They couldn't find their way home, and it was already starting to get dark. Lily needed to return home to her parents. If she didn't return in time, her parents would be scared. There was also the danger that in their search for her, they might throw away or break the statuette, which could prevent Lily from returning home. So, they were desperate to find a solution. They ran down a path that seemed familiar, but it was not the right way. They ran to the left, but that wasn't the correct path either. They climbed the trees to see further, but since it was already dark, they couldn't see anything. They called for help, but no one heard them. They started to cry, but that didn't help either.

Suddenly, they encountered a man. Overjoyed to finally have some hope, they asked him the way to the mushroom home. But the man almost laughed at them. How could he know where all the mushrooms in the forest were, and how could he know which was the home of these little girls? The poor girls had to continue their journey, crying. They kept walking along any path that seemed familiar, but they couldn't find the way home. Lily kept thinking about what might happen if her parents accidentally threw away, broke, or lost the statuette before she could find her way back. Would she ever be able to return to her world? These were questions that even her friend didn't have answers to.

As they were tormented by these questions and both were scared, they suddenly had an idea: What if they made a big fire that produced a lot of smoke? Maybe someone would see them and help them find their way home. Excited by this thought, they quickly started gathering branches for the fire and found two stones to create sparks. But the stones didn't make sparks big enough to ignite the branches, and it started to drizzle. Poor girls, they started crying again.

Walking along the path, crying, they suddenly encountered a dog who asked what had happened. When they finished explaining how they went to play in the forest and now couldn't find their way home, how they had asked a man but he laughed at them and couldn't help, and how they tried to make a fire but it started to rain, the dog smiled and said:

"Nothing is easier for me than to take you home. Wherever your home is, I can find it easily. Let me sniff you, then climb on my back and hold on tight. I will sniff at the path you took. It might not be the shortest way to your home since you probably didn't come here by the shortest route, but I can smell your trail and find the way to your house. Come on! Get on my back! There! Carefully, so you don't fall! Are you both settled? Hold on tight! Here we go!"

The dog, sniffing the path all the while, almost ran until they reached the mushroom house. You can't imagine the route they took. If someone had drawn their path, it would have looked like spirals, snails, and zigzags, with lots of extra distance covered. But their joy was immeasurable when they finally arrived home. They thanked the dog immensely for his help, marveled at how sometimes dogs are smarter than people and rewarded the dog with a phenomenally tasty dinner.

Lily was transported home by the wind as usual, and everything ended well. After this incident, Lily asked her parents to always take great care of her statuette, and no matter what, never to throw it away, never to break it, and always to keep it in a safe place. In the gentle embrace of the night, Lily's heart was filled with gratitude as she carefully held her beloved statuette. With each twinkle of the stars above, she sent out good thoughts to the entire universe from her heart brimming with love and gratitude.

The story and characters in this tale are fictional. The following historical truths are acknowledged: Pottery was independently discovered in various regions, with the oldest clay vessels in the world being associated with the Jomon culture in Japan, making them among the oldest pottery discoveries worldwide.

Göbekli Tepe

DID YOU KNOW THAT THE oldest complex of megalithic structures discovered to date is located at Göbekli Tepe, in present-day Turkey? In Turkish, "Göbekli Tepe" translates literally to "Potbelly Hill" or "Hill with a Belly." Do you know why it was named that way? Yes, I think you've already guessed it – it received this name from the locals due to its round shape, resembling a prominent belly rising in the surrounding landscape. But you cannot guess the story of the place, so let me tell you!

Once upon a time, in the era we call the Stone Age, there lived a lion. He was young, strong, and very handsome, and he got along very well with all the animals. He helped them when they needed assistance, and he protected them when they were in danger, so the animals trusted him. They asked him to be their king. He, of course, accepted. Everything seemed fine; the king continued to protect the animals in his kingdom from enemies. However, after a while, his servants began to disappear.

First, it was the duck that was supposed to prepare the king's bath daily, which was replaced by another duck. Then, a month later, the next duck disappeared as well. Some time passed without any ducks disappearing, but then the wild boar went missing. He was the guardian of the king's food store, but one night he vanished without a trace. He was replaced by another boar, who also disappeared without a trace.

The animals found it suspicious that animals of the same kind kept disappearing for a period. First, it was just ducks disappearing, then only boars, followed by oxen, and so on. None of them were ever found again, neither alive nor dead. The animals told the king about the mysterious disappearances, which he had also noticed since his closest servants were the ones disappearing. However, no one dared to accuse the king for fear of being punished. Time passed, and during this period, the animals built a palace with enormous stone pillars, a beautiful, round structure covered with wood and branches, topped with turf.

Once, a snake who also wanted to be king and was very envious of the lion, thought that if he discovered the secret behind the disappearance of animals from the king's court and told the other animals, they would immediately gather, kill the lion, and make him the king because he would be their savior. Being very clever, he quickly understood the situation and never doubted that the king was guilty.

One night, when everyone was asleep, he made a small tunnel in the ground and sneaked unnoticed into the lion's room, under his bed. And what do you think he found there? A pile of animal bones: gazelles, deer, boars, goats, but also an impressive number of birds, especially vultures and ducks. The snake didn't hesitate, took the bones, and quickly called a secret meeting with the animals. By morning, he had convinced them that the lion was responsible for the mysterious disappearances. He persuaded them to kill the lion. They all set out, led by the snake who coiled around the horns of a gazelle to get a better view of the scene. Very angry with the lion, they all shouted, carrying all sorts of weapons to take revenge on him.

But they didn't know that the king had another big secret. Not only did he secretly eat his servants, but he also had a rare talent that no one else possessed: if he plucked a whisker and blew it into the wind, he could wish for anything he wanted, and it would come true. As the animals came to kill him, making a lot of noise, he woke up and immediately understood the situation. He pulled out a whisker, blew it into the wind, and wished for all the animals, and even the few humans living nearby, to turn into stones. And so it happened. When the transformation was complete, he covered everything with earth, and that's how the hill in that place was formed. And the lion, as if nothing had happened, went off to find a new kingdom. And so, as night descended upon the ancient hills, the secrets of Göbekli Tepe remained shrouded in mystery, waiting patiently to be unraveled by those daring enough to seek its hidden truths.

The story and its characters are fictional. Historical truths are as follows: Göbekli Tepe is considered the earliest known example of monumental architecture on Earth. It is the oldest complex of megalithic structures discovered to date, dating back to the Pre-Pottery Neolithic period, approximately 9600 BCE. It was found approximately 22 km northeast of Şanlıurfa in Turkey, near the village of Örencik, on the upper reaches of the Euphrates River. The structures were built by groups of hunter-gatherers at the end of the Epipaleolithic period and the beginning of the Pre-Pottery Neolithic period. The site includes T-shaped pillars arranged in circular plans, with stone walls between them. At the center of each circle are two larger pillars. The pillars at Göbekli Tepe are adorned with numerous reliefs and carvings depicting a variety of images and symbols. Among these are animals, human figures, and abstract symbols.

The most common representations are of animals such as bulls, boars, foxes, lions, snakes, birds (such as vultures and wild ducks), and insects. These animals are often carved in relief and sometimes appear stylized or schematized.

Some of the sculptures depict parts of the human body, such as hands and arms. Also, some pillars feature representations of human figures, although these are rarer and often stylized.

There are numerous abstract symbols, including geometric shapes and other motifs that are not easily identifiable. These symbols may have religious or ceremonial significance.

Göbekli Tepe is believed to have been a cultural or religious center, not a permanent settlement. There is debate as to whether the space delimited by the pillars could have witnessed hunting rituals, initiation, and passage rites, spiritual gatherings, or funeral practices. "Göbekli Tepe" translates from Turkish as "Potbelly Hill" or "Hill with a Belly". This name comes from the round and bulging shape of the hill where the archaeological site is located. The name reflects the physical appearance of the terrain before archaeological excavations began.

The Trio of Çatalhöyük

ACCORDING TO SOME ARCHAEOLOGISTS, Çatalhöyük was one of the earliest urban settlements in the world, while others consider it to have been a dispersed village, arguing that it lacks several elements to be characterized even as proto-urban, let alone urban. Village or city, one thing is certain: Çatalhöyük is one of the most important Neolithic archaeological sites in the world, located in central Anatolia, Turkey.

In the vicinity of this settlement lived three friends: a bull, a wild donkey, and a small bird. Day by day, they roamed through fields and sparse forests of shrubs and trees, and their favorite spot was the banks of the Konya River. Here, they met every time they wanted to discuss something or play together. But not only did they play together, they also sang. The bull provided the bass, the bird sang various melodies she invented herself, and the donkey intervened only for special effects, usually in songs with comic lyrics; the audience laughed very hard at such moments. Over time, they became so famous in the forest that everyone knew them and came to their concerts. This trio, the bull, the donkey, and the bird, lived happily, but despite their great fame, they weren't too wealthy. They sometimes didn't have anything to eat.

Once, the three of them met a lizard, who told them something wonderful. It described the human settlement as if it were something extraordinarily beautiful, where animals are fed, they no longer have to search for food, and they have everything they need in abundance. The bull, the donkey, and the bird immediately thought of visiting the humans, and even staying there, if it was so good for them. However, being smart and cautious, they thought of sending someone to verify what the lizard had said, and in case it turned out that life with humans was as wonderful as the lizard described, then they would all go.

They thought about whom to send. It had to be someone brave, but not too big, so as not to be noticed by the humans, and so they decided to ask a frog to go visit the humans and check how the animals lived there. The frog agreed, especially since the bird promised her a fat fly if she checked how the animals lived with humans and told them.

The frog went to the human settlement. But since the walls of the houses were tall, some even had multiple floors, the frog couldn't get into the humans' houses, nor into the place where the animals were kept. She thought a lot about what to do, she was embarrassed that she couldn't get in, and she didn't want to miss out on the fat fly either, so she thought to make up something. The three of them wouldn't know whether she was telling the truth or not anyway. So that's what she did. She went back to the bull, the donkey, and the bird, and told them that with the humans, the animals had a golden life. They slept all day, food was brought to them five times a day, and what food it was, the most delicious dishes on earth! The bulls were scratched on their backs daily, the donkeys were pampered on their tails and lavished with attention, and the birds had their food brought to them on golden plates.

The trio was extremely pleased with the frog's description; the bull and the donkey immediately wanted to go to the humans and ask them to stay with them forever. The bird was also excited about the idea, but being cautious, she said to the others:

"Let's do another test, just in case there's any danger there and we perish. It's better to send someone else to see how the animals live with humans. Let's wait another day, but at least we'll be sure everything is fine there."

The others weren't too keen on the idea, but for the sake of the bird, they waited another day. Whom to send, they all wondered. Once again, they thought it should be someone who could sneak into houses without being noticed. They chose a snake, told him what they wanted from him, and eagerly awaited for him to leave, but more so, they awaited his return with good news.

The snake, being very cunning, went near the houses, where the women had placed some baskets of food. At a moment when they weren't paying attention, he slithered into one of the baskets and coiled up there, waiting in great silence to see what would happen. Shortly after, the women picked up the baskets and took them inside the house, without noticing that there was a snake in one of them. He stayed there until he heard noises from the humans, but when they went to sleep, the snake emerged from the basket and began to wander around. He moved from room to room, climbed the stairs, and even went through the ceilings into the next rooms.

Are you curious to know what he found in the humans' houses? Well, the interiors of the houses at Çatalhöyük were composed of multiple white-plastered rooms arranged around a central, often larger room. This central space had walls painted with all kinds of hunting scenes, including scenes where wild donkeys were hunted. The animals, in reality, were not kept inside the houses, as the lizard had said, nor even in stables. They were kept somewhere near the houses, without a roof to protect them from rain, cold, or heat, and the animals did not seem happy at all.

In the larger rooms, the snake found bull horns, which did not bode well for the animals. The snake immediately understood that it was not a good place for animals. But being sly, when he returned to the bull, the donkey, and the bird, he only told them good things about how the animals were kept by the humans. He made up all sorts of untruths about how well and happily the animals lived there, and he repeated some of what he had heard from the lizard to make it more believable. If two animals say the same thing, it is more likely to be believed than if just one says it. Why do you think he lied like that? Firstly, he was afraid the animals might beat him for the bad news he would have given if he told the truth. Secondly, he expected a big reward from the bull, the donkey, and the bird if he gave them very good news.

They once again received the good news with great joy and were eager to go to the humans. But the bird held them back again. She said that although she believed what was said, she still didn't trust the snake much. Everyone knew how sly he was. She asked her friends to send one more animal to investigate the place and tell them if the animals really lived as well with the humans as they were told. The others didn't agree, but for the sake of the bird, as they knew she was very wise, they agreed to stay one more day.

This time, they sent a hawk. The hawk didn't even bother to fly to Çatalhöyük. He made a circle in the air, flying just far enough to disappear from the horizon of the three animals who had sent him, and then quickly returned. He thought to himself, why should he tire himself out going all the way there? If two animals had said the same thing about how well the animals were kept by humans, who would believe him if he said otherwise? Probably no one. So, he returned and repeated the lies told by the lizard and the snake. The bull and the donkey were overjoyed by the good news brought by the hawk and immediately set off on their journey.

The bird could no longer hold them back. However, she found it suspicious how little time the hawk had spent away from them and how quickly he had returned. But she didn't have much time to think, as they were already approaching the humans' houses. She took a deep breath and, with all her strength, sped toward the humans' houses. She wanted to get there before her friends so that if something was wrong, she would have time to warn them of any possible danger.

As soon as she arrived, she saw through the roofs of the houses the bull horns on the walls, and she saw the animals tied up and unable to leave. In an instant, she understood the situation. She returned as fast as she could to her friends, who had already reached the humans' houses. She quickly told them what she had seen and urged them to go back home while there was still time. But they didn't even have time to decide whether to believe her or not, as a crowd of humans, armed with spears and axes, suddenly descended upon them, intending to hunt them.

The poor donkey and bull barely managed to escape with their lives. The donkey nearly lost an ear, and the bull lost a horn in his struggle with the humans. But they escaped and made it back home. For three days, they rested without doing anything, without talking to anyone.

But after three days, everything returned to normal. They formed their musical trio again and continued to roam the forest. This time, however, they sang not only fun songs but also songs that told the story of what they had experienced and how animals lived with humans. They became so beloved by everyone that they received food and gifts from all as a reward not only for their music but also for warning everyone to stay away from humans. And so, as their fame spread among the animals, humans could no longer hunt there and had to move to other lands where the animals were still unfamiliar with them.

Thus, the wise little bird and her friends saved the animals in the region where they lived, and Çatalhöyük became depopulated. In the end, the trio of the wise little bird, the donkey, and the bull became heroes among their kind, remembered for their bravery and cunning.

The characters and events of this story are fictional. Historical truths are as follows: Çatalhöyük is one of the most important Neolithic archaeological sites in the world, located in central Anatolia, Turkey. It was inhabited from approximately 7500 BCE to 5700 BCE, according to some archaeologists, or until 4500 BCE, according to others.

The settlement consisted of houses made of sun-dried mud bricks and timber beams, clustered around inner courtyards accessible by external stairs and roof hatches, with no streets or public squares. The dwellings contained several whitewashed rooms arranged around a larger central one, often adorned with painted walls, believed to have served as family shrines. Clay bull skulls with real horns were found here, and the murals painted in red, green, black, and yellow depicted bulls, deer, hunters, and dancers.

Archaeological excavations have revealed evidence of wheat, barley, lentil, and apple cultivation. Cattle rearing became increasingly important, while wild bull and onager (wild ass) continued to be hunted. Clay seals, used for sealing storage vessels and chests, were also discovered here, indicating the existence of clan-based ownership of material goods. The settlement is renowned for its clay female figurines, considered to have religious or fertility significance, embodying the Great Mother, while clay bull skulls with real horns are seen as symbols of masculine creative force. Graves were often located beneath the floors of houses, suggesting a close connection between the inhabitants and their ancestors.

About the Author

Alexeyev K. Zurga is a historian, art historian, and musician passionate about archaeology with extensive experience in excavations at various archaeological sites belonging to different cultures and epochs. With a fervent passion for research, Zurga is dedicated to sharing historical and cultural information with young people and adults in a way that encourages them to always distinguish between reality and fiction. Through engaging videos and books, Zurga aims to educate in an enjoyable manner while also stimulating critical thinking. Zurga believes that learning about the past should be both interesting and enjoyable. By blending education with entertainment, Zurga hopes to inspire a lifelong love for history and culture in the minds of learners, empowering them to think critically and engage with the world around them.

Read more at https://www.youtube.com/@kuzsovszkizurga5042.

9 798822 726446